that's SO raven

Tell It Like It Is

Adapted by Jasmine Jones
Based on the series created by
Michael Poryes
Susan Sherman
Part One is based on the teleplay written
by Beth Seriff & Geoff Tarson.
Part Two is based on the teleplay written
by Dava Savel & Carla Banks Waddles.

Watch it on

Disney PRESS

New York

Printed in the United States of America

First Edition
1 3 5 7 9 10 8 6 4 2

Library of Congress Catalog Card Number: 2004112663

ISBN 0-7868-4684-4

For more Disney Press fun, visit www.disneybooks.com
Visit DisneyChannel.com

Part One

Chapter One

Why do they have to make the hallways so depressing? Raven Baxter wondered as she and her best friend, Chelsea Daniels, walked down the crowded, dingy school hallway.

Raven cast an eye over the drab, olive-colored walls and gray lockers. A few posters announcing the student council elections hung on the walls. I mean, it's bad enough that we have to be at school, she thought. They don't need to throw salt on the wound.

"Please, Rae. It doesn't matter who wins the student council elections," Chelsea said, continuing the conversation they'd been having. "The president never gets anything done. We need a president who'll actually do something, you know? I mean, this place is falling apart."

The girls stopped at their lockers. Chelsea spun her combination and yanked at her locker door. It didn't budge.

"It's not that bad," Raven protested, yanking at her own locker. It didn't open, either. Raven shot Chelsea a knowing look. They'd been through this routine before—about five thousand times.

"Uno, dos, tres," Raven and Chelsea counted in unison. Raven whacked the wall next to the left of the row of lockers as Chelsea did the same on the right. They banged the wall once, twice, three times—then they kicked the bottom row of lockers. Simultaneously, all of the lockers in the row popped open, revealing everything inside.

Hmm, Raven thought as she peered at the collage of magazine photos taped inside the door of another locker. I didn't know Jimmy was so into the U.S. Women's Beach Volleyball Team. And Gina—man, she's got some suspicious stuff in here. Like, why would she need two copies of our history book? Makes you wonder. . . .

Chelsea frowned in disgust. "And Rae, look at these lockers," she said.

"Yeah, I know," Raven agreed. "It's horrible the way they just open up like that." She peeked into another locker and her eyes widened. Pay dirt! "Oh, girl, look! The new Mary J. Blige CD. I gotta borrow this one," she said, pulling it out and shoving it into her own locker.

Chelsea glared at her.

Guiltily, Raven put the CD back into the locker she'd taken it from. I was just going to borrow it, she thought defensively. I would have put it back . . . you know, eventually. If I remembered.

"Rae, you know, it would be so easy to get them fixed." Chelsea shut all of the other lockers, then dug around in her own locker for her books. "All you have to do is write a letter to the school maintenance department. It's right there in section G-42 of the student manual."

Raven looked at her. "There's a student manual?"

Chelsea rolled her eyes and slammed her locker shut.

Automatically, Raven and Chelsea held their notebooks over their heads as plaster rained down from the ceiling.

Oh, snap, Raven thought as she brushed it off the shoulders of her blue velvet duster. I *hate* looking like I've got plaster dandruff.

"Girl, you should just run," Raven said as she and Chelsea headed down the hall.

"Rae, there's no running in the school

halls," Chelsea replied. "Section I-19. Hallway do's and don'ts," she added chirpily.

Raven gave her friend a look. "I *meant*, you should run for student president," she explained. "'Do's and don'ts,'" she muttered to herself in disgust. I swear, Chelsea *looks* normal, Raven thought, eyeing her friend's striped sweater, jeans, and sparkly barrettes. But do normal people memorize whole sections of the student manual?

"I don't know, Rae," Chelsea said. "I'm not the kind of person people vote for. You know, you've got to be in the 'in crowd.'" Chelsea made air quotes around the words. "And who wants that?"

"Yeah," Raven agreed, then added under her breath, "I do."

"I don't know," Chelsea said again. "I mean, I know I'd be a really good president, but—"

Raven cut her off. "But what? Chelsea,

you know about all the problems—"

Just then, a foul odor wafted by Raven's nose. Ooh, now the atmosphere around here is *really* getting putrid, Raven thought. "And when you get elected," she added, "could you do something about that stench?"

It took a moment for Raven and Chelsea to realize that was no ordinary stench. It was so foul, so pungent, so brain-scramblingly disgusting that it could only be one thing. . . .

"Ben Sturky!" Raven and Chelsea cried.

They tried to run, but Stinky Sturky charged right past them. He stopped dead in front of the student council elections sign-up poster.

While his back was turned, Raven and Chelsea tried desperately to fan the stench away. Ben was a sweet guy, but he definitely didn't smell like it.

A moment later, Ben whipped around to

face them. Raven and Chelsea pretended to be fanning themselves, but Ben didn't seem to notice anything out of the ordinary.

"Student council elections," he said, a hungry gleam in his eye. "I think I'm going to run. I smell victory."

"Oh, we all do," Raven assured him, trying to breathe through her mouth. "I'm sure everybody does."

"Thanks!" Ben said brightly. "Rock the vote."

"How about 'wash' the vote?" Chelsea whispered to Raven as Ben hurried off down the hall.

More like deodorize the vote, Raven thought.

"You know, Rae," Chelsea said as she fell into step beside Raven, "I was thinking, I wouldn't be that bad at it." She hugged her books against her chest. "I could be a really good president. You know, I'm friendly, I'm loyal, I'm energetic . . ." Chelsea stopped in her tracks. "I just described a dog, didn't I?"

Raven bit her lip. "Yeah," she admitted. "But, you know, people love dogs." She put her hand on Chelsea's shoulder. "Think about it, Chels. You against Ben Sturky. You do the math."

Suddenly, Raven's hand went cold. The world began to spin. . . .

Through her eye
The vision runs
Flash of future
Here it comes—

What's this? I'm seeing a poster with the names BEN STURKY *and* CHELSEA DANIELS *written on it.*

Hey, check it out—it's the results of the

student council election! Looks like Ben got 187 votes. Who knew he was so popular?

Wait, wait! Now the number of votes for Chelsea is coming into focus. It looks like she got . . . three?

Oh, no!

My girl's gonna lose—to Stinky Sturky!

A moment later, Raven came out of her vision. She swallowed hard and glanced guiltily at her best friend. I just told Chelsea to do the math about beating Ben, Raven realized, but that equation doesn't add up the way I thought it would.

"Actually, math wasn't my very best subject," Raven mumbled quickly.

"Okay, Rae." Chelsea grinned, clenching her fists in excitement. "I want to do it. You totally convinced me. I want to run. Oh, I never would have thought about doing this if it wasn't for you. Thank you." She gave Raven a huge hug.

Raven felt like she couldn't breathe—and it wasn't just because of Chelsea's squeeze. How can I tell her that she's going to lose by 184 votes? Raven thought. It would hurt her feelings too much.

Okay, Raven decided, when in doubt, fake it. "Yeah, girl," Raven said uneasily. "What are friends for?"

Chelsea gave a quick wave and hurried off down the hall. Raven watched her go. She's so happy, Raven thought. So excited. So gung ho.

How in the world am I going to get out of this one? she wondered miserably.

Chapter Two

"**E**ddie, you should've seen this vision," Raven complained to her other best friend, Eddie Thomas, later that morning. "Chelsea got three votes, and Ben got a hundred and eighty-seven."

Eddie winced. "Well, did you tell her?" he asked.

"No, I couldn't do that," Raven admitted. "You know Chelsea. I mean, she'll take it all personally. I couldn't do that to her." She glanced toward the end of the hallway, where Chelsea was busily trying to hand out flyers to anyone who would take them. Not that anyone was taking them.

Raven smiled and shook her head. "Aw, look

how cute she looks passing out her flyers. Who wouldn't vote for that?"

"Hi, I'm Chelsea Da—" Chelsea started, but the guy she was talking to ignored her. She looked at the girl behind him. "Hi, I'm—" The girl kept walking.

"Hi?" Chelsea said to her back.

Frustrated, she turned to try another section of the hallway—and ran smack into the school principal, Mr. Lawler. Chelsea's flyers fluttered everywhere, as the ice cream Mr. Lawler had been eating flew off his cone and splatted onto the floor.

"My pistachio-praline triple scoop!" Mr. Lawler sprayed. He had a slight pronunciation problem—he spat his *p*'s all over anyone within a ten-foot radius. Which meant that anyone who got called into the principal's office tried to remember to bring an umbrella. Including the parents.

"Oh, Mr. Lawler, I'm so sorry!" Chelsea bent down and picked up the ice cream with her fingers, then squished it back onto the principal's sugar cone.

Look at Chelsea, Raven thought. What a problem solver! Okay, so it's kind of a disgusting solution—but, whatever works.

"No problem," Mr. Lawler said with a sigh as he stared down at his repaired dessert. "Oh, what the heck?" He took a bite of his ice cream and headed off down the hall.

Eddie grimaced. "How does she get two votes?"

"No," Raven corrected. "Three votes."

Eddie gave her a doubtful look. "I'm on the fence," he said.

"Okay, Chels, this is how it breaks down," Raven said after school that day. She, Chelsea, and Eddie were hanging out in the Baxters' living room, working on Chelsea's campaign.

Raven had decided that she didn't have any choice. Since she couldn't tell Chelsea the truth about her vision, she would just have to do everything she could to keep it from happening. So, Raven had appointed herself Chelsea's campaign manager, and she'd made Eddie her assistant. Raven promised herself she would do whatever it took to get Chelsea elected.

"In our school, there are sixty-four jocks, twenty-two nerds, sixteen hip-hoppers, and three Jamaican exchange students," Raven explained, using a long wooden pointer to indicate the colored pie chart she had made. "Now . . ." She cocked an eyebrow and looked at Chelsea. "In order to get their votes, you've got to speak their language."

"I mean, you gotta walk the walk," Eddie said as he strutted across the living room, looking supersmooth in his oversized red denim jacket and jeans, "and talk the talk."

"Or walk the walk and chit the chat," Chelsea said perkily, then started to giggle. "I just added my own little flair!"

And that's the kind of flair that loses elections, Raven thought. "Yes, you sure did," she told Chelsea with a smile. "Don't." Raven cleared her throat. "Okay, we're going to start with the jocks."

"Now, there's two things you gotta know, Chels," Eddie said. "You gots to keep it simple and you gots to grunt." He hopped off the couch to face Raven, pumped his arms twice, and flexed. "Yo," he said.

"Yo!" Raven replied, flexing in response.

"Yo! Yo!" Eddie and Raven squared off, and started Yo!Yo!ing like crazy. Then they grunted furiously and knocked shoulders.

Eddie grimaced.

"Ow!" Raven said, rubbing her shoulder.

Note to self, she thought, it's okay to sound like a jock, but that doesn't mean you have to get physical.

Just then, Raven's mom and her little brother, Cory, walked through the front door.

"Yo! Vote for Chelsea!" Raven shouted at them, pounding her chest. "Are we gonna win this thing? Are we gonna win this thing?"

"Yeah, Coach!" Eddie cried, ripping open his jacket. "We're gonna win this thing!" He let out a roar.

Mrs. Baxter and Cory gaped at them in shock as Raven and Eddie started marching around the living room, chanting, "Vote, vote, vote, vote, vote, vote, vote, vote!" Raven got so excited, she knocked over a vase with her elbow. She managed to catch it before it hit the floor.

"Hey, hey, hey, watch it!" Mrs. Baxter cried. "Your Aunt Lois is in that vase."

Chelsea leaped off the couch. "Yo, Mom!" she shouted. "Sorry, they're just helping me with my campaign!"

Did Chelsea just try to flex? Raven wondered as she watched her friend in full "jock" mode. Or is she planning to use that wild arm flapping to get the chicken vote?

"Vote for Chelsea! Go-o-o-o . . . Chelsea!" Chelsea ran in place for a moment, then planted her hands on her hips and grinned hugely. "That was my jock."

Mrs. Baxter smiled and nodded politely. "And it was very good," she said brightly. Then she leaned over and whispered to Raven, "Help her."

Raven nodded. I'm starting to see where my vision was coming from, she thought.

Cory strutted up to Chelsea, his crush-girl. "Well, you know you got my vote, baby," he said, waggling his eyebrows.

Chelsea patted him on the cheek . . . then stepped as far away from him as she could.

"Well, at least you know you have the round peoples' vote," Raven said, yanking her brother out of the way. "Okay," she announced, settling onto the arm of the couch, "we're going to work on the hip-hoppers."

"Oh, let me do that one," Mrs. Baxter said, switching into her best hip-hop accent. "We talkin' 'bout my girl Chelsea, here. I mean, she's in the heezey for sheezy. She's off the chain. She got my vote, she got my props, and she got . . ." Mrs. Baxter eyed Chelsea. ". . . my shirt." Raven's mother dropped her hip-hop voice. "What are you doing in my shirt?"

"Mom," Raven said, holding up her hand, "now, we're just using it for the campaign. No big deal."

"Yeah, home-mom," Chelsea piped up, popping up from her seat on the couch. "I was just borrowing your shirty bizurty. Because mine was all dirty bizurty." Chelsea stopped and looked over at Eddie. "Can you use the same word twice?"

Eddie walked over to Raven. "I'm off the fence," he muttered.

"Okay, Chelsea," Raven said quickly. "Maybe we should work on the Jamaican vote."

"Oh, now that one's easy," Mrs. Baxter said, slipping into a convincing Caribbean accent. "You want the Jamaican vote, child? Me tell ya how." She put her arm around Chelsea and gazed off into the distance, as though she was watching the sun set over warm blue Jamaican waters. "Come closer and listen to the island breezes—"

Raven smiled as she watched her mom. Okay, this one is going to work, Raven thought confidently. I just know it!

chapter Three

"Come closer and listen to the island breezes," Chelsea said the next day at school. She was wearing an orange-and-green batik shirt and a huge knit hat. She had her arm wrapped around a student wearing an African-print vest.

Raven stared at her friend in horror. What's worse? she wondered. Chelsea's hideous fake dreadlocks or her hideous fake accent?

Chelsea looked over at two more students with dreadlocks and Caribbean-style clothing. "Me thinks a vote for Chelsea is a vote for better lockers," Chelsea went on in her ridiculous accent, "new bike racks, and jerk chicken in the cafeteria, mon." She scrunched up her face and let loose with a chicken squawk. "Bok! Bok!"

Okay, that does it, Raven thought, hurrying over to grab her friend. "Hey, Chelsea, listen to me," she said quietly. "The Jamaicans are over there." Raven pointed to three kids wearing T-shirts, sweaters, and jeans at the far end of the hall. They waved.

Chelsea's eyes widened.

I guess the Jamaican vote is out of the question, Raven thought with a sigh. Oh, well. It's only three votes, right?

Then again, she added to herself, that would have given us twice as many votes as we have now.

Later that morning, Raven and Chelsea peeked into the computer lab. Sure enough, the nerds were there, working on . . . well, whatever nerds worked on in the computer lab. Raven glanced at her friend, who was sporting some serious geek glam. She had on a buttoned-up shirt, a pocket protector with about a thousand pens, and thick glasses. To top it off, her hair was in raggedy pigtails.

"All right, Chelsea," Raven said, slapping her friend on the shoulder. "Nerd votes. Go get 'em." She gave Chelsea a little shove.

Chelsea stumbled over to the first two nerds she saw. "Greetings, guys," she said, waving her hand. "Chelsea Daniels here to tell you to vote for me and I'll increase the volume of space in all your lockers." She laughed nervously, and gave a good nerd-style snort.

You go, you little nerd! Raven thought proudly. At least Chelsea's dork imitation was way better than her Jamaican one.

The nerds eyed her doubtfully. "Well," one of them said sarcastically, "since volume is length times width times height, and height is a constant, I severely doubt you can increase the size of our lockers." He looked around at his fellow geeks in triumph.

The entire computer cluster cracked up, hooting and snorting.

Chelsea shuffled backward, and Raven put her arm around her. "Oh, okay," Raven said to the nerds. "Keep that snorting thing going, guys. It really drives girls wild."

Okay, that's a big "no" on the nerds, Raven thought as she and Chelsea escaped into the hall. Maybe trying to get Chelsea to speak these people's language wasn't such a good idea, Raven realized. Something seems to be getting lost in translation. Something like *votes*.

Raven and Eddie sat at their usual table in the school cafeteria, watching as Ben Sturky hovered over a table of students nearby. The students were cringing—but only slightly. For one thing, Ben had his arms down at his sides, so he wasn't at maximum stench level. For another thing, the odor wafting from his grungy clothes was only slightly worse than the smell coming from the cafeteria kitchen.

"What can I do to get your vote?" Ben demanded.

Carter, a blond kid sitting at the table, shrugged. "It would be great if we had some better food around here."

Ben narrowed his eyes and smacked the table in determination. "I'm gonna march into that kitchen, and I'm gonna close the door behind me, and I'm gonna tell that cook—" The students drew back as Ben raised his arms. "'I'm not leaving here until you give us vegetables that are green and meat that's not!'"

Whoa, Raven thought, that's a powerful threat.

"He's got my vote," one of the girls said.

"Go, Ben," said another girl.

"Go, Ben!" the table chorused as Ben trotted off.

Eddie put down his sandwich in disgust. "Man, how are we gonna compete with that, Rae?" he demanded. "He's stinking his way to the top." He sniffed and shook his head.

"Well, he's not there yet," Raven countered. "We can't just give up and let Chelsea lose. She'll be totally humiliated." Adjusting her long pink sweater, Raven picked up her feather-topped pen and a notepad and marched over to the table Ben had just left. "Hey, guys," Raven said. "All right, before you vote for Ben, let me tell you some of Chelsea's ideas. Carter," she said, turning to him, "you know how the ceiling sometimes falls down on us? Well, it turns out it violates all these, like, laws and things. And Chelsea knows just who to complain to."

One of the girls shrugged. "I don't care about that."

"Really? Okay, Joy, what do you care about? Because whatever it is, girl, Chelsea will hook it up."

Joy held out two books. "I care about getting these library books back on time."

"Really?" Raven asked. She hesitated for a moment. Is that all it takes to get a vote around here? she wondered. "Well," she said slowly, taking the books, "it's a deal. If you vote for Chelsea." She slapped a VOTE CHELSEA sticker on Joy's shoulder. "Don't tell her," Raven added in a whisper.

"Cool." Joy smiled brightly. "I'll vote for her."

Raven nodded and picked up her notebook. "Okay."

A girl named Anna piped up, "If you walk my dog after school, I'll vote for Chelsea, too."

"Deal," Raven promised, slapping a sticker on Anna. "Just don't tell her."

Eddie hurried up to Raven as she made her way across the cafeteria. "Rae," he said, scowling, "what are you doing?"

"I'm getting some votes," Raven said defensively.

Eddie frowned.

"Hey, it's two more than we had," Raven told him. "What's a couple of extra chores?"

Besides, Raven was getting an idea . . . a seriously brilliant, campaign-winning idea. All she needed was a little help from Eddie.

"Just a couple of extra chores, huh?" Eddie said ten minutes later.

Eddie and Raven's lunch table was surrounded by kids. It turned out that practically the whole school was willing to swap their votes in exchange for a favor. Eddie stamped a piece of paper and handed it back to a girl holding a skateboard. "Okay, consider your wheels oiled. Vote Chelsea." He handed the girl a VOTE CHELSEA button. "Next."

"Okay," Raven said to another kid, handing over a receipt. "One tuba washed and buffed. Vote Chelsea. Don't tell her. Keep it moving, people. Keep it moving. Keep—"

Suddenly, Raven noticed that someone was coming her way . . . and it was the one someone she didn't want to see! Chelsea was walking toward Raven's table with a tray in her hands.

Raven scurried out of her seat. "Chels, girl, what are you doing here, sweetheart?" she asked, dragging Chelsea away from the table by the elbow.

Chelsea smiled, confused. "Rae, we always meet for lunch."

"You know, I've been thinking about that,"

Raven said quickly. "We need to mix it up. Get to see new people. And you know what they say. 'When you love someone, you gotta let them go.' I love you, Chels." She gave her best friend a gentle push. "Go."

Chelsea started to walk away, but stopped in her tracks when she noticed the crowd around Raven and Eddie's table. "Rae, why are all of these people lined up?" she asked, turning to face her friend.

"They're your public," Raven explained. "Everybody!" she shouted, turning toward the line. "I would like you to meet the new president of these United . . ." Raven thought for a moment. ". . . Classes," she improvised. "Chelsea . . ."

Raven paused. The people in line were looking everywhere—to the right, to the left. One guy was even looking at the ceiling! Raven had to swallow a snort of disgust.

"She's over here!" Raven whispered loudly, then shouted, "Daniels!"

A cheer went up from the group of students who were signing up for Chelsea favors. "Chelsea! Chelsea!" they chanted.

Chelsea grinned. "Wow, looks like things are starting to get better," she said to Raven. "I'm going to go get some flyers. Okay?"

"Okay." Raven gave a little wave as her friend took off. Then, with a deep sigh, she headed back to the table and slid into the seat beside Eddie. "See? You see how happy she is? And you know what? It really didn't take all that much work."

Carter poked his head through the crowd. "Babysit my little sister!"

Suddenly, the crowd erupted into a chorus of demands. "Vacuum my floor! Feed my parakeet! Clean my pool! Rake my yard! Wash my dog!"

"One at a time, people," Raven begged as the shouts kept coming. "One at a time, people, one at a time . . ."

Whoa, Raven thought as the kids buzzed around her, this campaign is getting seriously outta control. Am I a genius, or what?

Chapter Four

"Okay, one bike wash," Raven said into the phone as she ironed a shirt with her other hand.

They were only half-a-day into Operation Vote Chelsea, and so far everything was going smoothly. Well, sort of smoothly. Eddie was washing a large, fluffy dog in a tub on the Baxter's kitchen counter. And Raven had paid Cory ten bucks to help with the extra baby-sitting and laundry. But the votes were piling up, and Chelsea had no idea what was going on, so as far as Raven was concerned, everything was perfect!

"Vote Chelsea," Raven told the caller. She clicked the call-waiting. "Hello? Yes, it's true.

One vote for Chelsea gets you a favor. . . ." She glanced at Eddie and lowered her voice. "Yeah, sure, Eddie will take you out on Saturday."

Eddie looked up from his dog-washing duty. *"What?"*

"Oh, and he'd love to wear that," Raven said into the phone quickly. "Okay, bye. Vote Chelsea." She hung up.

"Wear what?" Eddie demanded. "And who was that, Rae?"

"Ah, I don't know," Raven told him, "but she's going to pick you up at eight. And wear your biker shorts."

Eddie narrowed his eyes at Raven. "Great. First, I'm a dog washer, now I'm somebody's boy toy."

"Eddie, listen," Raven said, "we do not want Chelsea to lose this election. You know how she gets when even one person doesn't like her. This is a hundred and eighty-seven people not liking her." Raven turned to the baby she had propped in a high chair and dangled a spoonful of baby food at him. "Come here, sweetie. It's good. It's yummy, see?" She took a bite of the baby food. Ooh, Raven thought, grimacing, that was a big mistake. "Okay, now I know why they feed that to people who can't talk. Come here, sweetie," she said, lifting the baby out of the high chair.

Cory walked into the kitchen carrying a huge tub of laundry. "For all this work, Chelsea's gonna have to break me off a little somethin' somethin'," he said.

Raven gave him a tight smile. "If you tell Chelsea about this, I'll break you off into a little nothin' nothin'," she replied as she patted the baby's back.

"Whoa!" Cory waved his hand in front of his face. "Stinky baby. I think his poop just pooped."

Someone rang the doorbell. "Cory, you go get the door," Raven ordered. "Eddie, come change this baby."

"Why do I have to change him?" Eddie demanded as he oiled a bicycle chain. He had decided to let the dog soak for a while.

Raven held out the baby. "Because I fed him."

"Exactly," Eddie said as he took the baby. "You fed him, so that means this . . ." He held the baby out so that his butt was in Raven's face. ". . . is your fault. All up in the booty area."

"I fill the top," Raven snapped, "you empty the bottom."

Out in the living room, Cory yanked open the front door. "Chelsea!" he screeched when he saw her standing on the front step. He slammed the door in her face.

Wait, Cory thought, it isn't a good idea to

slam the door in the face of the girl you like. He yanked open the door. "Sorry, babe," he said suavely, winking. Then he slammed the door shut again and ran into the kitchen.

"It's Chelsea!" he announced.

"What is she doing here?" Raven cried.

"Well, maybe she's dropping off laundry," Eddie suggested sarcastically. "I mean, everyone else in the world is."

Raven ignored him. "You guys change the garage, and put everything in the baby," she barked, striding toward the living room. Wait—did that make sense? Raven thought, stopping in her tracks. "Reverse that. Strike it. Okay."

Raven hurried to the front door. Play it cool, she told herself as she opened the door a tiny crack. "Hey, Chels!" she chirped, a big fake grin plastered across her face. "How's it going, girl?"

"Great!" Chelsea said with a smile. "I have my speech. Do you want to hear it?"

"And ruin the surprise?" Raven replied. "Never. Bye!" She slammed the door and started back toward the kitchen.

Chelsea knocked again.

Sighing, Raven went back to the door and opened it.

"How come everyone keeps slamming the door in my face?" Chelsea asked as she walked into the living room, flipping her now slightly bent index cards.

"Because, um, Cory is doing a science project," Raven improvised, "on, um, how many times somebody can get the door slammed in their face before they say something. Yeah, Cory," she shouted toward the kitchen, "she's a three!"

"Anyway," Chelsea said brightly, "want to hear my speech now?"

"Oh, girl, I would love to." Raven shoved Chelsea onto the couch and started toward the kitchen. Please tell me those boys have hidden the evidence! she thought desperately. "But I've got to go answer the phone."

Chelsea's brow wrinkled in confusion. "I didn't hear the phone ring."

"Right," Raven replied, "that's because I'm a psychic. I see the future." She gazed off into the distance. "Ding-a-ling-a-ling! There goes another one. I have psychic call-waiting, okay." She pushed open the door to the kitchen. "You guys," she whispered to Cory and Eddie, "I can't get rid of Chelsea. You guys have to get this stuff out of—"

Raven stopped and stared. Eddie was wearing safety goggles and a nose clip, while Cory had on a catcher's mask and oven mitts. Eddie brandished a pair of tongs at the baby, who was lying on the kitchen counter.

"Shh!" Eddie hissed at Raven as he stared down at the baby. "No sudden moves, Rae. We're trying to take him by surprise."

Rolling her eyes, Raven walked over to join the diaper busters. "It's a sweet little baby," she said.

"Sweet?" Eddie screeched. "That ain't chocolate in there!"

Raven reached for the baby's diaper. "All you do is take off these little tabs. Like this. There's nothing to it."

At that moment, the diaper stench hit them. Raven, Eddie, and Cory all fell down like they'd been punched in the face.

Woof! Woof!

Just then, the dog started barking. Raven, Eddie, and Cory hopped to their feet. Raven motioned to the boys that they should get the dog out of the house and hide as much of the stuff as they could. Then she raced back toward the living room, just in time to meet Chelsea at the door.

Chelsea tried to peek into the kitchen, but Raven blocked her view and slammed the door shut. "Is that a dog in there?" Chelsea asked. "Rae, I could've sworn I heard barking."

Raven grabbed her friend by the shoulder and led her away from the kitchen. "Oh, girl, that's just my cough." She let out a loud, hacking cough.

Chelsea shook her head. "No, it didn't sound like that," she said as Raven steered her onto the couch. "It sounded more like a dog barking. Like a real dog."

"Girl that's crazy." Raven flopped onto the couch next to Chelsea. "I don't have a dog."

"I know."

Just then, the still-wet dog that Eddie had been washing trailed through the kitchen door and hopped his front feet onto Raven's lap.

"Well," Raven said brightly, "have you met my dog?"

"Rae, you just said you didn't have a dog," Chelsea snapped.

"Um, I don't," Raven put in quickly. "You do. Happy birthday!"

Meanwhile, back in the kitchen, things were getting crazy, fast. "Here," Eddie told Cory as he handed him the wrapped-up stink bomb. "Take this dirty diaper."

Cory looked at the diaper with disgust. "What do you want me to do with it?"

"Toss it," Eddie said.

"Oh, okay." Cory tossed the diaper at Eddie, who caught it reflexively.

"I don't want it," Eddie cried, tossing it back.

Cory threw it again. "I don't want it!"

"I don't want it, either!" Eddie threw the diaper at Cory—a little too hard. It landed against the neon BAXTER'S PLACE sign that hung on the wall over the breakfast table. Sparks flew from the sign. The diaper stuck there, beginning to pop and sizzle.

"Ew . . ." Eddie crinkled his nose in disgust. "It's *cooking*."

Chapter Five

Back in the living room, Chelsea was getting frustrated. She couldn't figure out why Raven was acting so strange.

"Where are you going?" Raven asked her, racing toward the kitchen to block Chelsea's path.

"To get something to drink." Chelsea tried to shove her way past, but Raven didn't budge.

"Oh, I'll get something to drink for you! Don't worry about that, Chelsea!" Raven shouted, hoping that the boys in the kitchen would hear her. She reached her arm into the kitchen and felt them place something in her hand. Raven held it out to Chelsea. "Here you go."

Chelsea stared at the drink. It was a baby bottle full of milk.

How can I play this off? Raven wondered. "There," she said, shaking some milk from the bottle against her wrist. "I'll make sure it's good for you."

Chelsea looked at Raven like she thought her friend might be going crazy. "I was thinking something more like a soda," she said.

"Soda? Girl, did you know that stuff is bad for you?" Raven insisted, sticking her hand back into the kitchen and waving it frantically. "Milk brings strong bones. I'll even join you—" Someone put something in her hand and she pulled it back. It took her a moment to realize what she was holding. "—with a nice soda."

Chelsea snatched the soda from Raven's hand. "Thanks," she snapped, annoyed.

Please let something happen to get me out of this situation, Raven begged silently.

The doorbell rang.

Oh, thank you, Raven thought. "I'll get that!" she chirped. "You just sit down and take care of your new dog." Raven shoved her best friend onto the couch as she raced toward the front door.

But when Raven opened the door, her heart sank. There stood Anna—and her dog.

"Hey," Raven said in her perkiest voice, "what do you want?"

Anna held out the leash. "You said you'd take Buddy for a walk."

"How'd you guys get here?" Raven asked.

Anna shrugged. "We walked."

"Well, I guess my job is done," Raven said. "Vote Chelsea!" She gave a quick thumbs-up, before slamming the door in Anna's face.

Meanwhile, another person was knocking at the Baxters' back door. Eddie yanked it open. "Oh, man!" he wailed as one of his classmates handed him a bundle of joy, "Another baby?"

As if in response, the baby projectile vomited onto Eddie's face.

Cory started laughing . . . until the baby he was trying to diaper let loose with a missile of his own. Cory sputtered and waved his arms as baby pee landed all over him.

"Who's laughing now, little man?" Eddie demanded, cracking up.

Cory didn't even reply. Grabbing a pot lid, he used it as a shield against the fountain of pee.

Things were getting out of control, fast.

"Rae," Chelsea demanded, when Raven returned from the front door. "What is going on in the kitchen?"

"Nothing," Raven insisted.

From the kitchen came the distinct sound of a baby wailing.

"What was that?" Chelsea moved toward the door, but Raven wedged herself firmly in Chelsea's way.

"You know what?" Raven said, blocking the door with her arm. "First, you want to spoil your birthday present. And now, you want to ruin Christmas."

Chelsea's jaw dropped. "You got me a baby?"

"Some people would just say 'thank you,'" Raven told her.

"Rae, what is going on in there?"

"Chels, trust me," Raven pleaded, spreading her arms wide across the French doors. "You don't want to see what's going on in that kitchen." She knew that her voice sounded desperate, but there was nothing she could do about it—she *was* desperate.

"Wow," Chelsea said quietly. "Okay, Rae." She took a couple of steps backward.

Raven sighed with relief and stepped away from the door.

That was a major mistake. With catlike speed, Chelsea shoved past Raven and darted into the kitchen, where she stopped and gaped at what she saw. Eddie was sitting at the kitchen table, holding two babies. Cory was sitting in the dog's washtub, covered in bubbles.

"Wanna scrub my back, baby?" Cory asked, holding up a dish scrubber.

"Hey, um, yeah," Raven put in quickly. "So, Eddie just stopped by and brought us surfboards and some babies!"

"What is going on?" Chelsea cried.

Just then, Anna and Buddy burst in through the back door. "Hey, what's up, Raven?" Anna snapped. "We had a deal. If you don't walk my dog, I'm not voting for her." She jerked her head at Chelsea angrily.

Chelsea looked like she'd been slapped in

the face. "What is she talking about, Rae?" Chelsea asked, as Anna and Buddy stormed out. It took a moment for the truth to dawn on her. "Are you bribing people to vote for me?" Chelsea asked slowly.

Raven didn't answer. She couldn't. I can't believe I let this get so out of control, she thought miserably. Chelsea looked crushed—and humiliated.

"*Are* you?" Chelsea demanded.

"Yes," Raven admitted, struggling not to burst into tears. "But only because I had a vision that you were going to lose."

"Then why didn't you just tell me?" Chelsea asked.

Raven swallowed hard. "Because I didn't want you to get hurt."

"Yeah?" Chelsea asked. There was a catch in her voice as she added, "Well, how do you think I feel now?"

Raven didn't know what to say. A moment later, Chelsea turned on her heel and ran out the back door.

"Chelsea, please!" Raven called after her. "No, wait—Chels!"

But it was too late. Chelsea was gone.

Chapter Six

"**P**eople," Principal Lawler spat into the microphone in the school auditorium, "today the candidates will be presenting their platforms."

Sitting on the stage behind him, Chelsea watched nervously as his saliva sprayed across the first three rows. Even Lawler's sprinkling speech couldn't take her mind off of her rattling nerves. She had no idea what she was doing there.

Nobody wants to vote for me, Chelsea thought. Raven had to bribe them to do it! And now I have to make a speech, and I don't know what to tell them. They don't care about my ideas. All they care about is getting their surfboards waxed and their dogs washed.

"Why is that important?" Lawler sprayed on. "Because every one of us is a participant in the political process." His last sentence sent so much saliva flying that the microphone shorted out in a burst of sparks. The audience—especially the first three rows—burst into applause.

Unfazed, the principal stepped down into the audience. "No need to panic, people," he said. "I'll just have to project."

"Psst!"

Someone was hissing in Chelsea's ear. And she knew exactly who it was. "Go away," Chelsea told Raven.

"I called you last night," Raven whispered through the stage curtain. "You've got to talk to me sometime."

"No, I don't," Chelsea said through clenched teeth. "Go away."

"Come backstage."

Chelsea folded her arms across her chest. "No."

"I'll hit you," Raven warned.

Chelsea rolled her eyes. "You will not." A moment later, Raven's fist pushed out the curtain and walloped her on the back of the head—hard. "Ow!"

Chelsea didn't want to talk to Raven . . . but she wasn't about to sit there taking a beating from a stage curtain, either. She stood up and ducked backstage.

"What?" Chelsea demanded.

"Okay," Raven said, clasping her hands together earnestly, "I'm just gonna say it." She cleared her throat. "Bribing people was a very bad thing. And girl, from my heart, I'm really sorry. I'm really, really sorry. Okay, give me some love." Raven moved in for a hug.

But Chelsea didn't move at all, except to fold her arms across her chest. "You done?"

Raven gave Chelsea a pleading look. "I would be if you'd give a girl some love."

Huffing, Chelsea turned to go.

"Wait, okay. Chelsea, please," Raven begged.

Chelsea turned back. As mad as she was, she just couldn't walk away from her best friend.

"Listen, I didn't want you to get hurt," Raven explained. Her dark eyes were bright with tears. "I thought I was being a good friend."

"You don't have to protect me all the time," Chelsea told her. "I'm a big girl. So what if I lose by a hundred votes?"

"One hundred eighty-four," Raven corrected.

"Okay, I didn't need to know that," Chelsea said. Taking a deep breath, she went on, "It's disappointing, but I'll get over it."

"I guess I should've told you about the vision in the first place, huh?" Raven said.

Chelsea nodded. "But you didn't. And now I have to go out there in front of all those people, and I don't know what to say."

"Well," Raven said slowly, "what do you want to say?" She cast a sideways glance at Eddie, who was crouched by the curtain ropes. Go brilliant plan! Raven thought.

Eddie began to softly pull the ropes, dragging open the curtain behind Chelsea.

"I don't know," Chelsea said with a sigh. "I mean, part of me wants to tell them I quit. But then the other part wants to say that all bribes are off, but you should vote for me anyway, because I'd make such a good president. And I really care about this school."

Raven looked at the audience behind Chelsea. They were listening carefully—but Chelsea still had no idea. My girl is on a roll, Raven thought. All she has to do is say what's in her heart.

"Why?" Raven prompted.

"Why?" Chelsea repeated. She thought for a moment. "Because we spend more time here than we do at home, and we deserve a ceiling that doesn't fall on us and . . . and . . . and we deserve lockers that actually work right, and two lines in the cafeteria so we can get our food faster and actually have time to eat it. You know what, Rae?" Pressing her lips together, she shook her head. "None of that even matters now, because I'm not going to run."

"Are you sure about that?" Raven asked.

The audience burst into applause.

Chelsea's eyes widened as Raven gestured to the crowd behind her. Turning, Chelsea came face-to-face with an auditorium full of people—and all of them were cheering for her.

Raven and Eddie exchanged grins.

"Rae," Chelsea whispered, "what am I going to do?"

Raven smiled at her friend. "I can't watch your back all the time."

Chelsea hesitated a moment. Finally, she stepped to the front of the stage to address the crowd. "Hi," she said. "I'm Chelsea Daniels. And I want to be your president."

The crowd erupted into wild applause as Chelsea turned back to look at her best friends. Eddie gave her a thumbs-up.

Raven smiled. Finally, she thought with relief, one of my plans for Chelsea's campaign actually worked!

Chelsea smiled as another student posted the results of the student council elections. "Eighty-six!" she said, turning to Raven. "I guess I changed your vision."

"You sure did, girl," Raven said happily. Ben Sturky had won the election with 104 votes, a lot fewer votes than Raven had predicted.

"And you lost all on your own. I'm so proud of you," she added, pretending to wipe a happy tear from her cheek.

Just then, Principal Lawler skittered by, followed by the foul-smelling Ben Sturky. "We want more vending machines!" Ben cried.

"Done," Lawler promised, retreating from the stink.

"Increased library hours," Ben went on.

"Fine, fine," Lawler said quickly, backing away.

"And air-conditioning in the summer," Ben insisted.

"Oh, I can't," Lawler begged as Stinky Sturky forced him into a corner of the hallway, cutting off his escape. "It's a budget thing. It's impossible."

Ben lifted his arms, feeling the full weight of his presidential power. "We want it!"

"You got it!" Lawler shouted, flailing in the corner.

Ben grinned hugely. "Score!"

Raven and Chelsea exchanged smiles. Hey, Raven thought, I guess things didn't turn out so bad. Chelsea got an honest election, Ben got to be student president—and we're all getting air-conditioning in the summer.

But best of all, I got to keep my best friend, Raven thought as she wrapped her arm around Chelsea's shoulder. And that's really all that matters.

**Raven and Chelsea pretended to be
fanning themselves.**

**"In order to get their votes, you've got to speak
their language," Raven told Chelsea.**

"The Jamaicans are over there," Raven said.

"I would like you to meet the new president of these United . . . Classes," Raven improvised.

"Great. First, I'm a dog washer, now I'm somebody's boy toy," Eddie said.

"It's a sweet little baby," Raven said.

"Wanna scrub my back, baby?"
Cory asked Chelsea.

"You lost all on your own. I'm so proud of you,"
said Raven.

"I just had a vision that my parents are going to split up," Raven said.

"You can't spell 'we' with an *i*," Chelsea said.

"How do you know you didn't just bake it into that cake, or something?" Mrs. Baxter asked.

"This should keep them together for years!" Raven cried.

"Hi, Mom. Hi, Dad," Raven said.

"You come and take a seat right here,"
Chelsea said.

"Hello, folks, and welcome to Rusty's Bar
and Grill," Raven said.

"Your dad and I are not getting a divorce.
Not even close," Mrs. Baxter said.

that's SO raven

Part Two

Chapter One

"**O**h, look!" Raven sang happily as she followed the delicious smells coming from the kitchen. Her parents were standing together at the counter, whipping up breakfast.

"It's the perfect Sunday morning," Raven went on. "Dad's making waffles, Mom's squeezing fresh orange juice, and . . . well . . ." She cast a heavy look at the breakfast table, where her brother was sitting with his pet rat. "Cory is still living here. Almost perfect."

Cory glanced at his rat. "I know, Lionel," he agreed sympathetically. "She's mean. What?" He held the brown-and-white spotted rodent to his ear, then turned to Raven. "He thinks you're ugly, too."

"Cory, in the cage," Raven snapped. "You, not the rat."

The back door opened, and Eddie walked in carrying a duffel bag. "What's up, folks?" he called as he walked over to the waffle iron to inspect Mr. Baxter's cooking. "Your house-guest has arrived!"

"Hey, Eddie," Raven said. The rest of her family chorused hello.

"So, Eddie, what kind of waffles do you want?" Mr. Baxter asked. "We got blueberry, boysenberry, raspberry, and strawberry," he added in a goofy country-western accent.

Eddie peered into the waffle iron and waggled his eyebrows mischievously. "Okay, well—how about Halle Berry?"

Raven's dad hooted with laughter as he and Eddie slapped hands. "Don't hurt nobody!" Eddie called, guffawing. "Shake it up, shake it up!"

It took them a minute to realize that Raven's mother wasn't laughing. She gave them the evil eye from her place by the juicer.

"So, you're just going to have the plain waffle?" Mr. Baxter asked quickly.

Eddie nodded. "Uh, yeah."

Glancing nervously at his wife, Mr. Baxter started to work on the waffle.

"Yeah," Eddie said again as he hauled his duffel bag to the side of the kitchen. He decided he'd better change the subject—quick. "Oh, my mom told me to tell you guys thanks again for letting me stay here while she's at her dental conference."

"It's the least we could do," Mrs. Baxter said sincerely. "She takes care of our teeth, we take care of her son." She gave Eddie a hug. "You're family," she told him warmly. "Did you bring the free toothpaste?"

"Yeah." Eddie reached into the pocket of his

oversized black denim jacket and placed the toothpaste on the counter.

"Why don't you take your stuff upstairs?" Mr. Baxter suggested. "And when you come back down, you can have breakfast. You're going to be staying in Cory's room."

Eddie gave him a double thumbs-up. "Okay."

"What?" Cory screeched. "No way!"

Mr. Baxter frowned. "Cory," he warned.

"Fine," Cory said. "But if you cut the cheese one time," he added, pointing a warning finger at Eddie, "you're sleeping on the couch."

"Well, aren't you glad you're staying with my loving family?" Raven asked Eddie, who laughed as he followed Cory upstairs. She walked over to her parents and wrapped her arms around their shoulders.

But as soon as she touched them, everything went cloudy, and then . . .

**Through her eye
The vision runs
Flash of future
Here it comes—**

*Gosh, Dad looks really serious. And mad!
Why is he looking at Mom that way?
"That's it, Tanya," Dad says. "I can't take
this anymore. We're going to have to split
up."*

What?!

Pulling her arms away from her parents, Raven
glanced at her mom and dad. Is this vision for
real? Raven wondered. It has to be—they're
always for real. But that's terrible, because . . .
it means my parents are getting a divorce!

Chapter Two

"Oh, no, no," Cory announced as Eddie started to unpack his bag onto Cory's dresser. "Now let me explain the rules of my room. No gels." He tossed a tube back into Eddie's bag. "No smells." He tossed back a bottle of cologne. "No sprays, no—mouthwash?" Cory picked up the bottle of blue liquid and thought for a moment. Finally, he placed it back on his bureau. "You should keep that."

Eddie scowled at Lionel, who was perched on Cory's shoulder. "Is he gonna be staying in here?" he asked.

"That's the same thing Lionel just said about you," Cory replied. He went over to Lionel's cage and put the rat inside.

Just then, Raven walked into Cory's room. Her happy Sunday-morning feeling was completely gone. "Cory, I need to speak to Eddie alone," she told her brother.

"Excuse me?" Cory said, lifting his eyebrows. "This is my room."

Oh, no, Raven thought. I do not have time to be dealing with my little brother's attitude. But she decided that the best way to get rid of Cory was to humor him.

"Oh, that's right!" Raven said in a chipper voice. "Boy, and there is something so cool about your room."

Cory grinned, and Raven grabbed his hand and pulled him over to the door. "Come here and let me show you," Raven said, yanking Cory into the hall. "You'll love it. Stand out there. Ready?"

Cory nodded eagerly.

"Ready, ready?" Raven asked, backing into

the room. "Look. . . ." She shut the door in his face. "It locks."

Ignoring the banging coming from the other side of the door, Raven turned to her best friend. "Eddie, I am freaking out. I just had a vision that my parents are going to split up."

"Whoa." Eddie's eyes widened. "Your parents? They're the last people I thought would ever get a divorce."

"I know," Raven agreed. "I mean, they hardly ever argue that much."

"Hey, my parents never argued, either," Eddie replied. "So I never saw it coming. But you did, so you still have some time to do something about it. And I'll help you."

"I'm listening," said Raven.

"Okay." Eddie pressed his lips together in thought. "Well, there are always little signs when people are thinking about getting a divorce. Like, you know how your parents are all happy and stuff?"

Raven grinned. "Yeah."

"That's gotta stop," Eddie told her. "They're just holding in all that anger."

Raven gave him a doubtful look. "Well, you think? Eddie, I don't know . . . I think I might need a second opinion."

But who do I know that's qualified to give an opinion on my parents? Raven wondered.

"Well, Raven, you have come to the right person," Chelsea said later that day.

Okay, she doesn't exactly *look* like the right person, Raven thought, eyeing Chelsea's muddy smock. Chelsea smoothed her clay bowl with a sponge as it spun on the potter's wheel in front of her. On Sundays, Chelsea took a ceramics class through the arts club at the school.

"Both my parents are therapists," Chelsea went on, "and I can tell you, like, anything you want to know about relationships."

"Okay," Raven said, sitting forward on her stool, "what does it mean when—"

"Time's up!" Chelsea chirped. "See ya next week. . . ." She cracked up at her own joke, hooting madly.

Raven glared at her. Why did I think I needed a second opinion? she wondered.

"I'm totally kidding," Chelsea said, patting Raven and Eddie on their knees.

"Here's what I've been thinking," Eddie said, ignoring Chelsea's joke. "Maybe Rae's parents are going to break up because they haven't been spending enough time together." He shrugged. "I mean, that's what happened to my parents."

"Yes, yes," Chelsea said in what Raven guessed was supposed to be her "serious therapist" voice. "That's a good point, Eddie. A successful marriage is one that coexists with equality and mutual respect." She gestured broadly. "A couple should unselfishly put aside the 'I' and make more time for the 'we.' 'Cause you can't spell 'we' with an *i*." Chelsea grinned at Raven.

Why is Chelsea giving me that smug smile? Raven wondered. What she's saying doesn't even make sense! "You spell *insane* with an *i*," Raven pointed out.

Chelsea seemed to deflate a little bit.

"You know," Raven said, "maybe I just need to get my parents to spend more time together."

Eddie nodded. "Exactly."

"Yes, yes, yes," Chelsea agreed. "They call that creating a safe place for the 'we' to grow and to blossom. . . ."

Raven rolled her eyes. You call this help? she

thought. Reaching out, she squashed Chelsea's clay pot on the wheel.

Chelsea stared down at the clay blob in horror.

Eddie gave Chelsea a smug grin. "We call that the 'us' shutting up the 'you.'"

Raven smiled. At last, she thought, I think we're getting somewhere.

Chapter Three

"**H**ey, Mom," Raven said as she walked into the living room later that afternoon. Her mom was slumped on the couch with her feet up on the coffee table, reading a book.

"What are you doing down here all alone in the quiet?" Raven asked, perching on the couch beside her mother.

"Being alone in the quiet," Mrs. Baxter said. She looked at Raven, waiting for her to move, but Raven just sat there, smiling. Finally, Mrs. Baxter closed her book. "But that's all over now, isn't it?" she guessed.

"And you know what else is good reading, Mom?" Raven asked brightly. "A cookbook . . . which is in the kitchen with Dad." Taking her mother's hand, Raven pulled her up from the couch and led her toward the kitchen. "And I'm sure he'd love for you to spend more time with him." She gave her mother a gentle push. Guiding her toward the "we," Raven thought, remembering Chelsea's words. Maybe Chelsea's advice hadn't been so bad after all.

Mrs. Baxter hesitated in the doorway. "Really?" she asked. "He never told me that. Did he tell you that?"

Raven's smile froze on her face. "Well, kinda, sorta, not really, okay, buh-bye." She gave Mrs. Baxter a little shove into the kitchen and shut the door behind her. Then Raven pulled back the curtain on the French doors and peeked in through the glass.

"Hey, hon," Mrs. Baxter said as she walked over to her husband, who was chopping vegetables for that night's dinner. "You need some help cutting those veggies?"

"Sure," Mr. Baxter said, passing her a knife. "Love some. Here you go." He handed her a carrot.

Mrs. Baxter started slicing the carrot into thin rounds. "Look at us," she said, smiling to herself. "Cutting together. Reminds me of when I was little. I used to help Great-Grandma Izetta in the kitchen. She'd always say, 'I don't believe in all that fancy weighin' and measurin','" Mrs. Baxter imitated in her best old-lady voice. "'Just throw it all in. It'll chew.'"

Raven's dad laughed. "How would she know? She didn't have any teeth. 'I came into this world with no teeth,'" he joked, imitating Great-Grandma Izetta's gummy speech, "'and I'm going out the same way.'"

On the other side of the kitchen door, Eddie walked up behind Raven. "What's going on?" he asked.

"Take a look," Raven said triumphantly, gesturing to the glass-paned door. "They're spending time together. No way are they going to get a divorce."

Eddie crouched down and joined her at the glass.

"And I'd say," Mrs. Baxter was telling her husband, "'Grandma Izetta, you don't wear your teeth, you don't wear your bra. . . .' And she'd say, 'Child, I'm ninety-two. Trust me, nobody's lookin'.'"

Raven smiled to herself as she watched her parents laugh. Am I brilliant or am I brilliant? she thought. Oh, let's just say I'm brilliant.

Just then, Mrs. Baxter's glance fell on her husband's hand. "Where's your wedding ring?" she asked suddenly.

Mr. Baxter looked away nervously. "Oh, um . . . You know I don't like to wear it when I cook 'cause it always gets junked up with food and stuff." He dug around absently in the pockets of his zebra-striped cook's apron.

"Victor," Raven's mother said sharply, "it's not just when you cook. You don't wear it when you shower, when you take out the garbage . . ."

Raven bit her lip. Ooh, this isn't how it's supposed to go! she thought as her mother's forehead creased with frown lines. What happened to the laughing and the imitations of Great-Grandma Izetta?

"Baby, I'm sure it'll show up someplace." Ever so casually, Mr. Baxter poked through a pile of silverware lying on the breakfast table. The ring didn't appear.

Mrs. Baxter looked over at the tall chocolate layer cake sitting on the kitchen counter. "How do you know you didn't just bake it into that cake, or something?" she demanded.

"Tanya, I'm a professional chef," Mr. Baxter said. "I don't make mistakes like that."

"Just forget it," Mrs. Baxter snapped. "The ring is a symbol of our marriage, and you treat it like it's nothing." Turning on her heel, she stalked out of the kitchen.

Mr. Baxter looked after her uncertainly for a moment. Then he looked at the tall chocolate cake.

Suddenly, Mr. Baxter shoved his hands deep into the cake's rich, chocolaty layers, digging for the ring. He tore the cake apart, but the ring was nowhere to be found.

Raven sighed. This hadn't gone according to plan at all. She'd tried to bring her parents together . . . and they'd only ended up further apart.

"Man," Eddie said the next morning as he and Raven hurried down the stairs, "it's too bad your parents had that fight last night. That cake was looking good."

Raven stopped and shook her head. "How can they get divorced over a missing ring?"

"They're not divorced yet," Eddie pointed out. "You still have time to change the future. You gotta stay positive, Rae."

"Positive?" Raven shrugged doubtfully. "I don't know if I can, you know. I just can't fake something like that." Taking a deep breath, she shoved open the door to the kitchen. Her parents sat there sipping their coffee—in silence.

"Morning, Sunshines!" Raven bubbled. "Who's gonna have a good day today?" She pointed to herself. "We are!"

Eddie looked at her and whispered, "I said positive, Rae, not psycho."

"Hey, has anybody seen Lionel?" Cory asked as he walked into the kitchen carrying his empty rat cage. "He got out again."

"Ask your father," Mrs. Baxter said wryly.

"He knows all about things getting lost."

Mr. Baxter frowned down at his mug. "Is this coffee bitter?" he asked himself, taking a sip. "No." He turned and looked at his wife. "Must be you."

"Hey, now, hey, now," Raven said quickly. She yanked open the refrigerator door, grabbed two eggs, and held them up temptingly. "Why don't I make us all a loving family breakfast?"

"I'm not hungry," Mrs. Baxter snapped.

"Neither am I," Raven's father agreed, turning back to the newspaper.

"I am," Cory said brightly as he settled onto a stool. "Two eggs over easy," he ordered, pointing at a plate in front of him.

Glaring at him, Raven slammed the two raw eggs onto his plate. "Okay," she told her little brother, "dig in."

Cory stared at the eggs.

Hey, Raven thought, he's lucky I broke those eggs on the plate—and not on his head.

"Kids, I'm going to take you to school," Mrs. Baxter announced, hopping off of her stool. She grabbed her bag and headed for the back door. "I'll be waiting in my car."

Mr. Baxter hustled out of his chair. "No, no, no—" he insisted. "*I'm* taking the kids to school." He grabbed his keys and hurried toward the back door. "I'll be waiting in *my* car."

But his wife was too quick. She shut the door on him and raced to her car. Quickly, Mr. Baxter yanked open the door and dashed after her.

With a shrug, Cory grabbed his backpack and jacket and followed them.

Raven looked at her best friend helplessly. "Eddie, what do I do?"

"Well," Eddie said, leaning against the counter. "There's only one thing you can do." He raised his eyebrows. "How fast can you break your leg?"

Chapter Four

After school let out, Raven and Eddie headed over to the arts and crafts classroom. Chelsea was waiting for them. She was wearing a smock and had a large bucket of papier-mâché ready to go.

Chelsea sat Raven down on a chair and propped her leg up on a stool. Then she got to work.

"Okay," Raven said as she watched Chelsea wrap strips of white papier-mâché around her leg, "this is never going to work."

"I'm telling you, Rae," Eddie insisted, "when I broke my leg, my parents forgot all about their problems and focused their attention on me. It really brought them together."

"Okay," Raven said, "well, Chelsea, you really have to make it look like it's in a cast."

A goofy smile appeared on Chelsea's face. "Hey, Rae," she said slowly, "why doesn't your leg just audition for the school play? 'Cause then it'll be in a cast. Get it? A cast? Like a cast?" Chelsea started giggling like mad. "Isn't that funny?"

Raven and Eddie pretended to crack up for a moment, and then the smile dropped right off of Raven's face. "No," she said.

Chelsea stopped laughing.

I love my girl, Raven thought, but she's got to stop making these awful jokes.

"You know what?" Raven said suddenly. "My parents are really angry. Maybe I just need to break one more thing. . . ."

"This should keep them together for years!" Raven said with a huge grin as Eddie wheeled her toward the door of the art room on a dolly. After an hour of work, Raven was now wearing about forty pounds of papier-mâché in the form of a full-body cast. It's kind of like wearing a suit of armor, Raven thought, only not as shiny.

Raven winced as Eddie accidentally knocked her against the door frame. The body cast made her much wider than usual, and her arms stuck out from her sides. There was no way for her to go through the door straight on. At last, Eddie managed to maneuver the dolly so that she could squeeze through sideways.

But the minute Raven was out the door, a teacher walking down the hallway tripped over her feet.

"Sorry, Mr. Simpson!" Raven called as the teacher went sprawling, scattering his books across the floor.

As Chelsea darted ahead to open the heavy

hallway door, Raven's outstretched arm got caught in the strap of a girl's messenger bag. "I'm so sorry!" Raven cried as Eddie tried to turn the dolly . . . and ended up dragging the girl by the strap around her neck. Finally, Chelsea managed to unhook the strap. "Sorry," Raven said again. "There we go. All right. Bye."

"Oh! I am so sorry," Raven cried again as she knocked a pile of books out of another student's arms. Eddie wheeled her on. "Can't help you," she called back to the guy.

Raven had almost made it out the front door when Eddie caught sight of a pretty girl passing by. He looked over at her and smiled.

"Eddie," Raven said, her eyes widening. Two workmen on step stools were stretching a banner across the doorway. "Eddie, there's a ban—"

Eddie continued to smile at the pretty

girl. He wasn't watching where they were going.

"Eddie," Raven screeched, "there's a banner!"

Too late! Raven and Eddie crashed through the huge green-and-yellow banner. One of the workmen threw down his hat in frustration.

Hey, Raven thought, you aren't the only one having a rough day. After all, *I'm* the one in a full-body cast!

"I'm telling you, Rae," Eddie said as he and Chelsea propped Raven up beside the Baxter's fireplace, "when your parents see you like this, they're gonna freak."

"Yeah, Rae," Chelsea agreed. "I mean, they're going to be up all night worrying about you. They won't be able to sleep or eat. I mean, their lives are going to be this bottomless pit of misery until you get better."

Raven grinned. "Promise?"

"Absolutely," Eddie said. "They're gonna come back together. We'll be upstairs."

Chelsea and Eddie darted up to Raven's room.

"Hey, Dad," Raven said, practicing her tragic look. "Hey, Mom."

Just then, a familiar, furry face appeared at the edge of the fireplace mantel.

"Hey, Lionel," Raven said to her brother's pet rat, "what are you doing here?" Lionel scampered along the edge of the mantel and up Raven's arm. "Lionel," Raven said gently, "you need to get back in your cage, sweetie."

Suddenly, Lionel leaped onto the neck of Raven's body cast. "What are you doing?" Raven asked nervously as the rat started to explore the edge of the cast. "Lionel, Lionel, Lionel." The rodent ducked inside the cast. "Lionel, get out of there!" Raven screeched, wiggling away from the squirmy rat. "Lionel. No, Lionel! Stop it!"

She shook the cast as hard as she could, but she couldn't move very well. Okay, Raven thought, I'll have to hop. Maybe I can get him to run out. She jumped a few steps, but that only sent Lionel further into the cast. Suddenly, Raven realized that she couldn't reach the mantel. There was nothing holding her up. . . .

Crash! A cloud of plaster dust flew into the air as her cast broke into a thousand pieces.

"No!" Raven cried.

Raven coughed on the plaster dust as she lay on the floor, flat on her back. "Dang it," she said miserably. Not only was her plan to get her parents back together ruined—now she was going to have to vacuum up all these plaster chunks.

Perched on her chest, Lionel looked down at her. Dumb rat, Raven thought, glaring at the rodent. Why couldn't my brother have a normal pet?

Just then, keys jingled in the lock. "No," Mr. Baxter said to Mrs. Baxter as he strode through the front door. "I said I was going to pick him up!"

"Hi, Mom. Hi, Dad," Raven said weakly from her place on the floor.

Neither of her parents even noticed her. Cory trailed in behind them.

"I think you're doing this just to get on my nerves," Mrs. Baxter snapped as she followed her husband up the stairs. "By the way, you're doing it quite nicely."

"Bye, Mom," Raven called weakly as her parents stormed up to their room. "Bye, Dad. I—I'm fine!" she shouted. You know, just in case they're worried, she thought.

Cory stared down at Raven, wide-eyed. "What happened to you?"

"Oh," Raven said, touched by her brother's concern. He actually looks worried! Raven thought. "Well—at least somebody cares. I was trying to help people out," Raven explained, "and see, and then . . ."

Leaning over, Cory picked Lionel up. "Did the bad lady hurt you?" he asked, glaring at his sister.

Raven rolled her eyes. Why didn't I see that one coming? she wondered.

Chapter Five

"I love this picture of me and my folks," Raven said, half an hour later. She was sitting on the floor of her bedroom, flipping through an old photo album as Eddie and Chelsea looked over her shoulder. "Don't we look happy?" Raven asked wistfully.

Chelsea peered at the photograph. "Where's Cory?"

"Oh, he wasn't born yet." Raven pursed her lips. "That's why we were so happy." She heaved a deep sigh. "Guys, I'm never going to stop this vision from happening."

"Look, Rae," Eddie said gently, "if it makes you feel better, divorce isn't so bad. Check this out. I've got two homes, two bedrooms, and two TVs. 'Course, a brother's gotta make two beds." He shrugged his shoulders. "But that's cool."

Chelsea's eyebrows drew together, like she didn't really believe what she was hearing. "Eddie, you're okay with your folks not being together?"

"No," he admitted, "but I deal with it." He looked down at the floor. "And I still think I could've stopped it."

Raven looked down at her photo album. I just can't believe that all of my parents' happy memories are over, she thought sadly. There has to be a way to make them see that they belong together. Like, look at this picture of them at the beach. They seem so in love! And this one . . .

Raven held up the album so that her friends could see. "Oh, you guys, look at this one," she said, pointing to the photo. "Mom and

Dad at a country-western bar. It was their first date."

Mr. and Mrs. Baxter were sitting at a round table in front of a fake cactus. They both had eighties-style hairdos and huge smiles.

"Oh gosh, they were so happy," Chelsea said.

Raven looked at her.

"And still are," Chelsea added, realizing her mistake. She patted Raven's shoulder. "Yes, and will be. Uh-huh, and, and, and . . . please stop me," she begged.

"Oh, no, Chelsea," Raven said quickly, "that's a great idea! All we have to do is remind these two people how much they still love each other."

"Yeah," Chelsea agreed.

Mom and Dad have just lost track of all the memories they've shared, Raven thought. All I need to do is give those memories a little jog, and the good feelings will come flooding back!

Raven smiled at her friends. *And I know just how to make that happen. . . .*

"What are you doing home so early?" Mrs. Baxter asked her husband as she walked up to the door of their house.

"I got a message from Rae," Mr. Baxter explained. "She said to get home right away."

Mrs. Baxter frowned as she dug around in her purse. "She left the same message on my cell. Do you have your key?"

"Why?" Mr. Baxter asked with a smug little smile. "Did you lose yours?" Grinning, he reached into the front pocket of his jacket, pulled out his key, and unlocked the front door. "It's okay. Happens to all of us," he said, gesturing for his wife to pass through.

She rolled her eyes.

"Uh . . ." Mr. Baxter said as he walked into the living room. It looked like it had been redecorated by a crew from *Trading Spaces*—the Texas edition. The Baxters' furniture had been replaced with bales of hay, western blankets, a giant cactus, and a small stage with lights in the shape of a horseshoe. Even the doors to the kitchen had been replaced by swinging saloon doors.

"What's going on in here?" Raven's father asked.

Eddie, dressed in a checkered shirt, a wide-brimmed straw hat, and a pair of overalls, burst through the saloon doors. "Howdy do, folks," he said as he strode across the living room followed by Chelsea, who was wearing a hideous purple dress with a ruffled skirt and a hat covered in fake flowers. Eddie took the stalk of hay from between his teeth. "Come on in."

Mrs. Baxter frowned. "Eddie, what is going—"

"No, no—no time for chitchat, Missy!"

Chelsea cried in a down-home Southern accent. "You come and take a seat right here." Chelsea guided Mrs. Baxter onto a wooden chair at a round table covered in a red-and-white checked tablecloth. "Just like you did on the night of June 23, 1983," Chelsea said.

"When you were young and in love," Eddie added, whooping, "wee-doggy!"

"June 23?" Mrs. Baxter thought for a moment, then turned to her husband. "That was our first date."

"It was?" he asked.

Mrs. Baxter glared at him.

Clearing his throat, Mr. Baxter nodded quickly. "It was."

"How 'bout somethin' to wet your whistle, huh?" Eddie suggested. "Hey, Jimmy Ray!" he shouted toward the kitchen. "Get on out here."

A moment later, a pint-sized cowboy in a ten-gallon hat and furry chaps burst through the saloon doors. "Howdy, pardner," Cory said to Mr. Baxter as he set two giant mugs of root beer onto the table. "Evenin', ma'am. Fine night for fallin' in love, ain't it?" he said to Mrs. Baxter, chomping on his gum.

The Baxters ignored that comment. "Okay," Mrs. Baxter demanded, "where's your sister?"

"Chelsea Mae," Cory called, "hit the lights."

Chelsea turned off the overhead light, and Cory adjusted the spotlight so that it was shining directly onto the stage.

"And now," Eddie said as he took the stage, "without further ado, introducing the little lady with the big voice and even bigger hair. Put your hands together for the queen of country music, Miss Rodeo Raven!" He and Chelsea let loose with a series of Texas-style whoops and cheers.

The curtain parted, and Raven stepped onto

the stage wearing a tall, blond beehive hairdo. She had on a sparkly, powder-blue outfit with white fringe and a matching blue cowboy hat perched atop her enormous hair.

"Hello, folks," Raven said into the microphone, "and welcome to Rusty's Bar and Grill, located on I-94 right next to Leanna's Hair Emporium." She whipped out a bottle of hairspray and began touching up her beehive. "Where the bigger the hair, the more we care." Raven grinned at her parents as she put aside the hairspray. "Are the memories of love just flooding back?"

"Flooding back!" Eddie and Chelsea chorused.

Mr. and Mrs. Baxter looked confused.

"Anyway," Raven went on, "here's a song for all you first-daters out there. Remember when love was new?" she murmured into the microphone. "And you loved him?" She patted her father on the shoulder. "And he loved you?" She patted Mrs. Baxter on the back.

Eddie hit the tape recorder, and a bouncy country-western beat started to play. *"Stay together!"* Raven sang.

"Stay together!" Chelsea and Eddie repeated, dancing around.

"You were meant to be," sang Raven, *"like white leather . . ."*

"Like white leather!" Chelsea and Eddie chorused.

"On Elvis Pres-ley! 'Cause love is rare . . ."

"Time will prove it!"

"Like my hair!" Raven patted her giant blond 'do.

"You can't move it!"

"No, you can't!" Raven crowed. *"Stay together!"*

"Stay together!"

"Like chili and corn bread." Raven put her arms around her parents' shoulders. *"Love's*

forever! Listen hard to what I've said. Remember this night. Try not to fight. And we'll be all right. Stay together!"

Eddie and Chelsea joined in, "Stay together!"

And all three friends sang the last line. *"For the sake of the kids!"*

"Stay together, please," Raven said quickly. She shoved her parents closer, until they were cheek to cheek. "Thank you!"

Once the song was over, Chelsea turned the overhead light back on. Mr. and Mrs. Baxter shared a long look. What does that look mean? Raven wondered. Are the memories of love flooding back? Or are they just wondering where I found this giant blond wig?

"You know what they're trying to do, don't you?" Mr. Baxter said to his wife after a moment.

Mrs. Baxter nodded. "They want us to stop fighting."

Mr. Baxter nodded. "Uh-huh. And they want you to apologize to me."

"Excuse me?" Raven's mother's eyes flashed angrily.

"Oh, one more time!" Raven cried quickly, starting up her song again. *"Stay together!"*

"Rae, c'mon," her father said, "please."

Raven froze in her tracks. Her heart hammered in her chest. I guess this song isn't having the effect I'd hoped, she thought.

"Now look, baby," Mr. Baxter told Raven, "we appreciate what you're trying to do, but you've got to let your mother and me work this out amongst ourselves."

"There'd be nothing to work out if you hadn't lost the ring in the first place," Mrs. Baxter told him. There was an edge in her voice.

"That's it, Tanya," Mr. Baxter snapped, finally losing his cool. "I can't take this anymore. We're going to have to split up."

Raven felt as though she had just been stabbed in the heart. "Eddie," she whispered, "that's my vision."

"You look upstairs," Mr. Baxter told his wife. "I'll look downstairs. One of us has got to find it."

Mrs. Baxter nodded and started toward the stairs.

"What?" Raven stared at her parents. "Eh, ah, um. Excuse me?"

Her parents turned and looked at her.

"I'm sorry, um—" Raven's eyes narrowed. "You're not getting a divorce?"

Raven's parents looked horrified. "A divorce?" they said in unison. They gaped at Raven.

"See," Raven said, "I had a vision of Dad saying, 'split up,' and that's what I thought." She blinked back the hot tears that were pooling in her eyes. "And I've been trying to keep it from happening."

"Oh, honey," Mrs. Baxter said gently, pulling her daughter into a hug. "Come here. Listen." She sat down next to Raven and took her daughter's hand in her own. "Honey, your dad and I are not getting a divorce. Not even close. Just because we have an argument doesn't mean we're not going to work things out."

Mr. Baxter leaned in so that he could look his daughter in the eye. "Yeah, and baby, you've got to understand, just because we disagree, it's not your job to fix it."

Mrs. Baxter looked over at Cory and wrapped her arm around him. "And that goes for you, too." She turned to Raven. "Okay?"

Raven smiled in relief. "Okay."

Raven had never been so grateful to have

her family around her. And I'll never take them for granted again, she swore silently. Well, except maybe for Cory.

Eddie heaved a sigh. "I'm glad that's over," he said, pulling off his straw hat and inspecting it. "This hat's messing up a brother's 'fro." He patted his head, inspecting the damage, and rolled his eyes. "Oh, bizzle."

"Funny," Chelsea said to the Baxters, dropping her crazy Southern accent, "I never really thought you guys would be into country-western."

Mr. Baxter put an arm around his wife's shoulders and they both started to laugh.

"Actually," Mr. Baxter admitted sheepishly, "we're not. I thought I was taking Rae's mom to 'Motown Night,' and it turned out to be 'Hoedown Night.'"

"That was the worst first date ever," Mrs. Baxter said. Then she looked up at her husband and added, "And I loved every minute of it."

"Really?" Grinning, Mr. Baxter leaned down and gave his wife a kiss.

Raven smiled. See? she thought happily. The memories of love did come flooding back! I guess my plan kind of worked, after all!

"Wee-doggy!" Mr. Baxter said playfully. "C'mon partner," he told his wife. "I'll go rustle up some vittles in the saloon. You too, Johnny Ray," he said to Cory.

"It's Jimmy Ray," Cory corrected. "Don't you recognize me, Daddy?"

Eddie turned to Raven as the rest of her family trailed into the kitchen for a snack. "I'm glad everything worked out for you, Rae," Eddie said gently.

"Thanks," Raven told her friend.

Eddie started toward the stairs.

"Oh, and Eddie," Raven said, "you know you couldn't have done anything."

Turning back, Eddie looked at Raven carefully. "About what, Rae?"

"About your parents splitting up," she explained.

Eddie didn't look convinced.

"I mean, didn't you hear what they said?" Raven went on. "It's your mom and dad's problem, not yours."

"I guess so," Eddie said slowly. "I just never really thought of it that way. Thanks, Rae." He gave Raven a hug.

A goofy smile spread over Chelsea's face. "Hey, guys," she announced, "I'm going to wear my outfit to school tomorrow because then, if I forget my homework, I could just say, 'My wee-doggy ate it!'" She waited for a response. "Get it? My wee-doggy? My doggy? Isn't that funny?"

Raven and Eddie pretended to crack up, then chorused, "No!"

Chelsea's face fell.

Dang! Raven thought. She has got to get some new jokes. Still, you don't have to be psychic to know that isn't going to happen anytime soon.

Chapter Six

"**H**ey, look what I found," Cory said the next morning as he ran down the stairs and into the kitchen.

Spotting the flash of gold in Cory's hand, Mr. Baxter grinned. "My ring!" he cried, putting it on his finger.

"Where did you find it?" Mrs. Baxter asked.

"I didn't," Cory explained. "Lionel did. It was in his cage sitting in a big pile of rat poop."

Grimacing, Mr. Baxter hurried over to the sink and started vigorously scrubbing his hands.

"Honey," Mrs. Baxter said to Raven, "do you mind walking Cory to school today?"

"No," Raven replied, "but I need a leash. And can you please make him promise not to lift his leg up every time he sees a bush?"

"Hello?" Cory snapped back. "I'm the one walking with the dog."

"You know," Mrs. Baxter put in, "your dad and I thought you might feel this way. But we still think that you should . . ."

Mr. Baxter flipped on the tape recorder, and a country-western beat bounced through the room. *"Walk together!"* Mrs. Baxter sang in a twangy Southern accent.

"Walk together!" Mr. Baxter hollered. He bounced up and down, tweaking his elbows out to the sides.

"You two were meant to be," Mrs. Baxter sang, *"like brother and sister!"*

"Brother and sister!"

"Why, you're a family!" Mrs. Baxter swung her arm in an aw-shucks gesture. *"Don't fight,"*

she cooed. *"It ain't right. You oughta be tight!"*

"Walk together!" Mr. Baxter chimed in.

"Okay, okay, all right, all right. Let's go," Raven said, scurrying toward the door. She grabbed Cory's arm as her parents hooked arms and swung, then skipped around in a do-si-do. As Mrs. Baxter swung close to Cory, Raven dragged her brother away from the crazy hoedown. "Hurry up. Don't let her touch you!"

"Yee-haw!" Mr. and Mrs. Baxter cried as they whooped and stomped to their own country song. "Woo-hoo!"

I really was wrong about my parents, Raven thought as she hurried out the door. They could never split up. They're two of a crazy kind!

Gaze into the future and take a sneak peek at the next *That's So Raven* story. . . .

Adapted by Kimberly Morris
Based on the series created by
Michael Poryes
Susan Sherman
Based on the teleplay written
by Jeff Abugov & Michael Feldman

"All right, class," said Mrs. DePaulo, "before you clean up, I have an announcement to make."

Raven Baxter tried to look politely inter-
ested and hoped Mrs. DePaulo wouldn't take
ten minutes to announce that it was Tapioca
Appreciation Month or something like that.

Mrs. DePaulo pulled something from under
her desk and plopped it on her head: a Viking
helmet with two long, blond braids attached.
She pushed it firmly down over her own hair
and smiled. "What does this say to you?" she
asked.

Eddie Thomas raised his hand. "You got
drafted by the Vikings?"

The class broke into laughter.

Mrs. DePaulo smiled tightly. "Funny. Cute."
She leaned over Eddie and glowered. "Quiet."

"Okay," Eddie agreed meekly.

Mrs. DePaulo looked out over the rows of
students with her helmeted head held high.
"Now, although I teach science, my first love
has always been opera. What do they have in

common?" She paused a moment. "*Nothing!* And that's why I'm bitter."

Raven and Eddie exchanged a confused look. Where was this going?

"Which brings us to the annual Festival of the Classical Arts," Mrs. DePaulo continued.

Ohhhhh, Raven thought. She whispered a warning to her best friend, Chelsea Daniels, "Here it comes."

Mrs. DePaulo's eyes scanned the classroom. "Who wants to sign up?"

It was major duck-and-cover time. Every student in the room dove under their desk in search of imaginary pencils, keys, and lost contacts.

"You get a beautiful trophy," Mrs. DePaulo coaxed.

Under her desk, Raven held her breath. For once, she didn't want to draw any attention to herself. Who cared about a stupid trophy?

"And a hundred-dollar gift certificate donated by the Bayside Mall," Mrs. DePaulo added.

A hundred-dollar gift certificate! Raven and everybody else came out from under their desks like groundhogs ready for spring. Raven and Chelsea gathered their books and stood up along with the rest of the class. The room was full of excited chatter.

"Hey, Rae, what do you think?" asked Chelsea as the students filed out. "Should we sign up? Are you getting any psychic vibes?"

Raven tried to look deep inside herself. She felt the room grow silent. Time seemed to stand still.

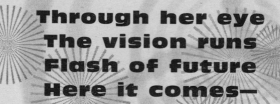

Through her eye
The vision runs
Flash of future
Here it comes—

I see . . . I see . . . I see . . .
I see nothin'!
Squat. Zip. Doodle. Nada.

Raven snapped back to the present. She refused to be disappointed. "No. I got nothing. But I *do* have an idea. We're going to do an opera."

Chelsea gave her long red hair an impatient shake. "An opera? Rae, c'mon. We don't know anything about opera."

Raven hugged her books and struck a "can-do" attitude, standing tall in her new denim jacket and matching boot-cut jeans. "Girl, we love the mall, and DePaulo loves opera. Therefore, we love opera."

"You do?" Mrs. DePaulo appeared suddenly next to them. "Wonderful!" she exclaimed, beaming. Her pen hovered over the clipboard, ready to sign them up. "So, Raven, what will you and your sidekick be performing?"

Raven was searching her brain for an answer when she heard Chelsea begin to sputter. "Wh-wh-what do you mean, 'sidekick'?"

Mrs. DePaulo looked up from the clipboard like she thought it was a dumb question. "Sidekick. You know. A follower. Hanger-on. Second banana."

Chelsea's face fell.

Bitter was one thing, Raven thought, mean was something else. Mrs. DePaulo was basically calling Chelsea a loser. Raven immediately moved closer to her best friend. "Mrs. DePaulo," she said in a firm tone. "Chelsea and I, we're equal bananas."

She felt Chelsea stand a little straighter. "That's right," she echoed.

"As far as what our act will be, all our decisions will be made together," Raven went on. She lifted her chin. Chelsea did the same. Raven motioned to Chelsea to follow her.

"Chelsea, we're leaving." She brushed regally past Mrs. DePaulo.

"Right behind you," Chelsea echoed.

Uh-oh!

Mrs. DePaulo gave them a smug look. Chelsea's little echo had just proved that she was second banana, like it or not.

Get Cheetah Power!

the Cheetah Girls

TV
G
Bonus Material
Not Rated

Now on DVD and Video

Buena Vista
Home Entertainment

Distributed by Buena Vista Home Entertainment, Inc., Burbank, California 91521. © Disney

a COMEDY SERIES
THAT'S aHEaD OF ITS TIME
PHIL OF THE FUTURE
DISNEY CHANNEL
ORIGINAL
WEEKENDS aT 7PM|6C
DISNEYCHANNEL.COM